Pioneer Lady
of
Southern Appalachia

Best Wishes
Darrell R. Fleming
aug. 6, 2016

by
Darrell R. Fleming

Table of Contents

Preface I
About the Author II
References and Resources III

Chapter One
    Hopes and Dreams 1

Chapter Two
    Pioneer Wanderlust 6

Chapter Three
    The Journey Begins 9

Chapter Four
    Surprise Meeting 13

Chapter Five
    A Good Day's Journey 17

Chapter Six
    Close Encounter 19

Chapter Seven
    Up and Over the Blue Ridge 22

Chapter Eight
    Trade 28

Chapter Nine
    Appalachian Spring 33

Chapter Ten
    A Pioneer's Illness 38

Chapter Eleven
    Friendly Pioneer Greeting 45

Chapter Twelve
 The Western Frontier Border 50

Chapter Thirteen
 An Unexpected Challenge 54

Chapter Fourteen
 New Beginnings 58

Chapter Fifteen
 Establishing a Wilderness Homestead 61

Chapter Sixteen
 Alone In the Wilderness 65

Chapter Seventeen
 Delayed Returns 69

Chapter Eighteen
 Welcome Home 74

Chapter Nineteen
 Pioneer Lady 81

Preface

Mary Jane Mullins Fleming, March 15, 1815 - October 6, 1893, became the first pioneer lady at the age of fourteen to settle in Clintwood, Dickenson County, Virginia in 1829.

To capture the indomitable spirit of this pioneer lady one must delve into the past to search for historical facts and, at the same time, realize the early pioneers' life stories were seldom written down. Instead, they were retold from generation to generation; therefore, different versions are often found. Yet, in these differences strong consistencies still remain in many of these stories. Exact times, dates, and places were often difficult to confirm but enough were found to establish some historical facts. These were included and became the foundation on which this story is based.

Therefore, the historical record of Mary Jane Mullins Fleming has been embellished through the author's research, travel, personal knowledge, and experiences to present a perspective of her real and imaginary story. Thus, a creative historical fiction emerged to assist in preserving the history and heritage of an important part of the author's family as well as Appalachian history.

With the aforementioned in mind, it is the author's sincerest hope that the reader will enjoy this account and have a deeper appreciation for the early pioneers and Mary Jane Mullins Fleming, Pioneer Lady of Southern Appalachia.

About the Author

Darrell Fleming grew up in Clintwood and graduated from Dickenson Memorial High School in 1953. He graduated from Union College in Barbourville, Kentucky with majors in English, History and Political Science and then received a Master of Education Degree in Secondary Education from The University of Virginia in Charlottesville.

After serving in the United States Army in Germany, he began teaching in Fairfax County Public Schools, Fairfax, Virginia. He taught high school English nine years, served as assistant principal, sub-school principal, and principal at the secondary level 16 years, completing his career as Coordinator of Human Resources for Fairfax County Public Schools before retiring in 1988.

His first book, *Family, Friends, and War Heroes*, was published and released in September, 2005. It is based on his Dad's diary written aboard a destroyer escort while serving in the Atlantic and Pacific theaters of World War II. The first print, a hard back with dust cover, was sold out. A second print, in soft cover, is available from www.darrellfleming.net and Amazon.com.

Darrell and his wife, Kathy, moved from Loudoun County, Virginia to Blountville, Tennessee in 1994. He enjoys reading, writing, promoting Appalachian authors and literature, traveling, golfing, and fishing.

References and Resources

The author used multiple sources to research information for the compilation of dates, places, and events included in Pioneer Lady of Southern Appalachia. He read, made notes, and used them to weave into the creative stories presented in this volume. As a result, it was difficult to give accurate credit to the many articles, journals, historical records, and books used. Therefore, a list of primary contributors is presented to inform the reader and assist future researchers and writers in their efforts to preserve history.

Avery County Historical Museum. *Burke County Land Records, 1779-1790*. Vol II. [Newland, NC].

Avery County Historical Museum. *Burke County Land Records, 1751-1809*. Vol III. [Newland, NC].

Dickenson County Heritage Book Committee. *The Heritage of Dickenson County, Virginia, 1880-1993*. Vol I. 1994.

Dixon, Danny. *Pathfinders, Pioneers, & Patriots*. Vol I. 2001.

Gentry, Tom and John Hartley. "Shouns Crossroads." *Mountain Electric Cooperative Publication* [Mountain City, TN]. March 2000.

Hughes, Jr., I. Harding. *Valle Crucis, A History of an Uncommon Place*. 1995.

"Mullins Descendants Urged to Contribute." *The Cumberland Times* [Clintwood, VA]. 29 February 1968, Thursday ed. p 1.

"Marker to Honor Lady Pioneer." *The Dickenson Star / Cumberland Times* [Clintwood, VA]. 6 October 1993, Wednesday ed. p 1-b.

"Pioneers of . . . Dickenson." *The Cumberland Times* [Clintwood, VA] 21 December 1967, Thursday ed. p 7.

Staley, Estelle. *Descendants of Robert Fleming and Elizabeth Stembaugh / Betty Stumbo*. April 1990.

Sutherland, Elihu Jasper. "The Mullins Family in Dickenson County." *The Cumberland Empire*. October 1932.

Sutherland, Elihu Jasper. "Some Sandy Basin Characters." 1962.

Sutherland, Elihu Jasper and Hetty Swindall Sutherland. *Pioneer Recollections*. 1994.

Waxman, Leanne. "History in the Raw at Trade, Tenn." *The Tennessean* [Nashville, TN], The Associated Press.

Wells, Leigh Ann. "Elkhorn Celebrates Daniel Boone." *Appalachian News-Express* [Pikeville, KY]. 28 May 2006, Sunday ed.

Chapter One

Hopes and Dreams

A crescent moon was descending on jagged Appalachian peaks in the early gray morning just before sunrise. Morning dew was beginning to give way to a rising mist forming over the little community of settlers on the banks of the Toe River in the Spruce Pine area of western North Carolina. This was early spring of 1829 when the urge to move to a more promising frontier took hold on an entire family.

Most of the older folks in this and surrounding settlements had left caring families and forgotten hopes behind in far away homelands of Ireland, England, Scotland, and other Western European countries. They dared to venture out for new hopes and dreams and a life of promised freedom, opportunity, and improved welfare for their future families. They endured turbulent ocean voyages on crowded ships for nine weeks or more to come to this new country, entering mainly through New York and South Carolina. Upon arriving and planting their feet on solid ground many continued their quest through rough and rugged wildernesses. They followed crude, muddy trails blazed by herds of eastern buffalo, Indians, long hunters, and adventurers to this isolated frontier community.

Some would remain here to till the soil and raise their families while others would choose to venture further, still seeking their elusive hopes and dreams. Many of those who moved on followed Daniel Boone, the great explorer of unchartered western territory, into the rich hunting grounds of what is now Southwestern Virginia, Northeastern Tennessee and Southeastern Kentucky. It was a beautiful and bountiful region so inviting to those who dared to venture forth.

John Wesley Mullins was a resident of this backwoods settlement. It is believed he began his journey in Northern Ireland, possibly Belfast. Although it is difficult to trace his country of origin because of the numerous Mullins families living in the colonies of Virginia, North Carolina, and South Carolina at this time. However, in 1790 under the newly formed Constitutional Representative Republic of the United States, a federal census listed him and his wife, Jane (Jennie) Bailey, with seven children living in Burke County, North Carolina.

Many hand-me-down stories by generations that followed John Wesley referred to him as "Buttin' John" because in his younger years he was quite a fighter and butted his opponents with his head to gain an advantage during the conflict. Also, while living in the Burke County area he voluntarily joined Colonel William Campbell's Over Mountain Men and fought in the Battle of Kings Mountain, South Carolina on October 7, 1780 where he helped defeat a much larger and better equipped British force led by the arrogant Major Patrick Ferguson. This act of bravery gained him the respected nickname of Revolutionary John which stayed with him the remainder of his life.

One of John Wesley's sons was also named John. He married Ollie Cox in Burke County. They, like their parents, began their family in the same settlement by farming and raising chickens, hogs, cattle, and horses on a small farm by the river. It was a quiet, peaceful life far removed from the rapidly expanding eastern coastline cities and towns that were bulging with new immigrants. The immediate area around the Spruce Pine settlement had plenty to offer a young growing family but the lure of owning a larger tract of more desirable land which lay westward over the mountains was ever present with John and Ollie.

In 1810, with the birth of his first child, David, young John and his brothers, James and Solomon, began discussing the possibility of exploring this region. They had heard about it from returning hunters and adventurers. What is more important, they wanted to investigate the possibility of relocating their families. Also, they needed to supplement their growing families' food supply which was necessary because of the steady stream of pioneers arriving from the East in search of the same hopes and dreams. Therefore, hunting parties had to venture further and further from the Toe River to find more plentiful game. It was on one such hunting expedition in the fall of that year that they discovered bountiful game and virgin territory which stretched westward from the Clinch and Guest rivers to the foothills of the Cumberland Mountains and eastward to the Breaks of the Big Sandy River as it entered Kentucky.

Once they arrived at the foothills of the Cumberland Mountains, their travels took them from the headwaters of the Pound River eastward to the Breaks. Not only did they find good hunting for bear, deer, elk, and turkey but also fertile valleys tucked neatly among the heavily forested hills. It had plentiful creeks and rivers abundant with fish, beavers, muskrats, minks, and the gangly, unattractive but very skillful fisher-bird, the whooping crane.

The hunting and exploring ventures continued for several weeks during which they had an occasional meeting with a few long hunters pushing through from the Wilderness Road and newly settled Washington and Russell counties of Virginia into the vast expanse of the Kentucky and Ohio territories. The brothers observed this migration and concluded that it would not be long until the area would be claimed by one of these. It was during this expedition that they began to believe their dreams of owning a large tract of land could come true.

After being away from the family longer than any other previous time, John's mind drifted back to the warmth and comfort of home. He came to the conclusion that he had sufficiently gathered enough meat to sustain his family during the approaching winter and began his return trek before the first snowfall. His brothers did not return with him; instead, they decided to claim land on the headwaters of the Pound River and remain for the winter to prepare cabins for their families to join them in the spring of 1811.

Having arrived safely home in early November with enough wild game to provide for the cold winter months, John received a joyous welcome by his family. The children were eager to hear about his trip and he promised to share stories with them during the long winter months when they gathered around the warm hearth. Ollie, too, was interested in finding out about the land and its potential for their future.

John settled back into the routine of living a contented life as a pioneer farmer on his small North Carolina property. However, as time moved slowly by and even years passed, his mind began to wander back to the area he had visited almost twenty years earlier. Besides that, more settlers were moving into the area along the Toe River and several were slowly making their way into Kentucky. So, after spending another unusually cold winter in the growing settlement and not being able to cast aside his hope and dream of owning a larger piece of virgin land, he and Ollie, after many discussions, made the decision to move their family to the area he had visited years before.

He knew from experience and what he had heard from his brothers, who returned to gather their families and dispense with their cabins and land, that it would be difficult to move the entire family and belongings on the first trip. In addition, he remembered the rough terrain and knew it would be a slow journey due to winter thawing and spring rains. Based on his best estimate, it would take about two weeks for a small family to make the trek with sufficient supplies to establish livable quarters and enough livestock to sustain the entire family when they arrived. Therefore, well thought out plans had to be made for Ollie and the children who would remain in North Carolina and for those who would accompany him into the unsettled region.

Chapter Two

Pioneer Wanderlust

It was a clear morning in mid April with frost on the high ridges and an early spring chill in the river valley below. At the first crow of the rooster, John arose, changed into his buckskin pants and shirt, and pulled on his hunting boots. He proceeded to stir the smoldering embers in the large open stone fireplace and added several small pieces of kindling to get a blaze going. He then put on some split logs to provide not only warmth in the cabin but also necessary heat for preparing a hearty family breakfast. Ollie got up, slipped out of her long cotton gown and into her handmade dress, donned her apron, leather moccasins, and followed him into the kitchen to begin preparing the meal.

Soft long twirls of smoke began to rise from the chimney of the cabin and fill the settlement with the smell of hickory wood from the open fireplace. Soon Ollie was preparing salt cured ham, eggs, homemade biscuits, and redeye gravy for the four members of young John Mullins' family who were about to depart for "a more promised land."

Ollie continued making the special breakfast which also included their favorite dish of fried apples smothered in fresh butter. She even made extra helpings to put on biscuits with ham and taken with them on the first day's journey. Working quietly in the kitchen, she began thinking about the difficult and uncertain venture being undertaken by her strong husband and three children. Also, she thought about the responsibilities resting on her shoulders of seeing to the planting and raising the large gardens on their small farm, caring for the animals, as well as the safety and well being of the seven other children. Life would not be easy for her in his absence but she was committed to the same hopes and dreams as her husband. Besides, he had described the freshness of the land, fullness of the streams, the peace, and quiet of the lush valleys so many times she could imagine it as if she had been there.

Mary Jane, who had just turned fourteen on March 15 and was excited about leaving with her father and brothers, busied herself helping her mother in the kitchen and performing last minute inventory checks on food supplies, cooking utensils, and other essentials. She paid special attention to wrap and store several gourds which contained different condiments required to make her meals more savory. One of these gourds contained sulphur to be used in preserving fruits and vegetables and in bleaching as well as disinfecting cuts and abrasions. She was an attractive young lady, small of stature with bountiful energy and a true pioneer spirit. Also, she had been well trained by her mother for the role of a strong woman needed to take on the many tasks she would face in the days ahead. Like her mother, she moved quietly about the cabin, giving careful attention to each detail to ensure her responsibilities were in good order for departure.

When the hearty breakfast was set on the large walnut table, Ollie sent Mary Jane to call her father and two brothers to eat. John, David, and Isaac were ready, having finished seeing to their preparations. They quickly washed their hands in the wash pan just outside the cabin door and took their places around the family table. This being their last meal together as a family until an uncertain future time, John offered prayer for their bountiful blessings. He concluded by asking God's protection on Ollie and the children while he was away and requested travel mercies for him and his three children that they would be led to a desirable place for the family to grow and prosper.

As they ate, conversations were more serious than usual. Ollie was making sure the children had completed their last minute chores, especially Mary Jane. John was going over a mental check list with the boys. It was evident to everyone around the table that there was excitement in the air and a strong urge to get started. When breakfast was finished, John dismissed the children to tend to their duties outside and make ready to depart. This gave him and Ollie time to exchange last minute thoughts about what to do in their absence from each other as well as to express their love and devotion. He promised to send back word of their progress when he found travelers and hunters returning to North Carolina. It wasn't necessary to give assurance that their hopes and dreams for a better life lay ahead because they had committed to that in many previous discussions. With a tender kiss and strong embrace in the warm kitchen, they confidently made their way outside to their children.

Chapter Three

The Journey Begins

"David, you got the horses hitched up and everything on the dray tied down?" John asked as he came out of the cabin, "It's going to be a long, hard climb up the mountains for a couple of days."

"Yeah, Pa. They're hitched and everything's tied tight and ready to go." David responded with an air of confidence. He was the oldest at nineteen and feeling a degree of responsibility for the party's welfare and safety.

"Isaac, how about the cattle and hogs? You fed and watered them before we move out?" John inquired of the youngest member who was only twelve years old.

"Yeah, Pa. They're looking pretty spry this morning," Isaac replied, as he watched the collection of animals and kept them gathered in an enclosed area.

"How about you, Mary Jane? You made a last minute check on the supplies to make sure we've enough to get us through to Trade? We'll resupply there for the rest of the trip. You know it's probably going to take the better part of three days to get there."

"Yes, Pa. Mommy says we have plenty for three days. She even made us some ham and fried apple biscuits to eat along the way."

"Okay," John continued, "let's say good-bye and move out before the sun gets any higher. It's already seven o'clock and the sun's going to warm things up pretty quick 'cause there's not a cloud in the sky."

Ollie began up front with David and gave each of her children a motherly hug and words of reassurance. She concluded by admonishing them to look out for each other and always follow their father's instructions. Then she strode over to John, took his hand and began walking toward the road leading to the mountains they must cross. John instinctively knew what she was saying by the tender touch of her hand and gave the call to "move out." Ollie walked a short distance with her husband and then, without speaking, loosed her grip from his and turned toward the cabin.

The small family of early pioneers waved a good-bye and began to move slowly away from the cabin. In planning his travel route, John had talked at length with his father who had been hired in the 1790's and early 1800's to help lay out and build a road all the way to the Tennessee state line. He advised him to take the road along the Toe River to the confluence with Roaring Creek because most hunters and pioneers who had gone before followed the river since the climb was more gradual. From there they would continue to follow the road to the top of the mountain where iron ore was being mined.

David led the way by driving a team of draft horses and keeping their household possessions, carpentry tools, and farming implements secured on the dray. He also had placed his trusty rifle and extra ammunition in a convenient location just in case he might need to ward off rogue bears or other wild animals.

A young bull and two cows were tied with ropes to the lead dray because the other cattle and hogs would follow them more easily. Isaac's responsibility was to keep the drove moving with his hickory staff as a prod. Besides, he was young enough to chase them back in line should they balk or attempt to stray.

John drove a horse pulling a smaller dray with

provisions, household items, and a dozen chickens in a wooden coop. He felt more comfortable carrying his rifle strapped over his shoulder just like he had on many hunting trips before. The family's two black and tan hounds joined in the steady pace moving back and forth among the travelers as if their duty was to alert their master to any impending and unforeseen danger lurking on the trail.

Mary Jane would bring up the rear by leading a horse with a large pack strapped across its back containing their clothing and other personal items needed for the arduous days ahead. She also brought along a heavy blanket to throw across the horse's back just in case she or Isaac got tired and needed to ride a spell. As they moved slowly away, she would occasionally steal a quick glance back to the cabin and see her mother standing on the porch. Then they gradually dropped over the ridge of the first hill and into the forest of the Blue Ridge Mountains which rose to more than 4,000 feet above them.

John had impressed upon his children the importance of establishing a steady pace which not only would help the animals stay together but also keep them on schedule. In addition, for a good part of the way they would follow the road traveled by the Over Mountain Men back in 1780 on their way to defeat the British in South Carolina and, therefore, finding a campsite would pose no problem. Their pace had to be about two to three miles an hour in order to reach Trade on the third day, which he estimated to be about forty to fifty miles away. There they would replenish supplies, make any necessary adjustments and repairs, and take a rest before forging on toward their intended goal.

John kept a close eye on Isaac to see how he was holding up and was pleased with his work as a drover. He looked back at Mary Jane to make sure she was keeping up. Then he surveyed the sun's position and estimated they had been traveling three hours and should have covered at least eight miles. He called up to David a couple of times to ask if he needed relief since he had a tough job setting the pace and making sure the dray was still in good shape.

David was a tall, handsome, and strong young man like his father and felt proud to have been chosen to take the lead. He declined his father's offer and kept moving at a steady pace. John, however, knew that it would be good for everyone, as well as the animals, to take a rest. He called to David again and told him to find a suitable place for a break where they could get water from one of the mountain streams and some shade.

They traveled only a short distance when David pulled the horses into a cool, shady hollow that had a stream tumbling over rocks with a sizable pool of clear water at the base near the road. This was a good place to refresh themselves with a splash of water on their faces and get a cool drink from the waterfall. The pond provided plenty of water for the animals.

Mary Jane led her horse to the pool for a drink before the others unhitched. Then she tied it to a small tree and began unwrapping ham and fried apple biscuits.

When they had taken care of the animals, rested, and enjoyed the snack, John and David went to examine the horses' hooves and shoulders for damage which might have been caused by the rough road and collars. They were in good condition and ready to go. They resumed their positions again and quickly regained their pace.

The sound of the rushing river traveling downstream was a constant companion and getting smaller as they steadily climbed upward.

Chapter Four

Surprise Meeting

    They had traveled about an hour up a particularly steep incline when David called back that someone was coming down the trail. He began to look for a place to move over and allow the approaching party to pass. He pulled into a wide place in the road made by an erosion of rocks and mudslide and the others closed up behind him. This gave them another welcomed rest from the ups and downs of the wagon road as it wound its way along the river.

    They were eager to meet anyone coming from that direction to find out what to expect further up the trail and took positions to greet them. As the oncoming party neared, John was surprised when he recognized one of the riders as his brother, James "Doc Jim" Mullins. He had remained in the Pound River area in 1810 and in 1815 purchased two hundred acres of land there. James had returned to the settlement only twice since then and that was to sell his farm and move his family.

    James, too, was surprised when he saw John. He knew from the drays and drove of animals that he had finally made up his mind to leave North Carolina. He quickly dismounted and rushed to greet his brother. The reunion was a happy occasion since they hadn't seen each other in several years. Then James called the handsome young man who was traveling with him to his side and proudly introduced him as his son, William. John, in turn, introduced his children. After exchanging greetings, the brothers began inquiring about each other's health and general well-being and their respective families. James was especially interested in his father, John Wesley. After all, he explained, one main reason he and his son were going to visit the settlement was to convince his father to come live with him since he was a widower and approaching eighty years old.

"He's been living with us for the past ten years or so since mother passed away," John informed him. "He's slowed down considerably but still in good health for his age. And I've about convinced him to come live with us when we get settled in Virginia. It appears that he's just about ready to do that."

"That's good news," James smiled, "I'll go directly to your house as soon as we get there."

"Oh, by the way," John interjected, "tell Ollie that everything's going just fine and the children are holding up well, especially Mary Jane."

While the brothers continued catching up for the years of absence, David began asking William to describe where they lived and what it was like. He wanted to know about the availability of land and farming conditions. William gave assurance that there was plenty of land still available. He told him about the grazing meadows near the river and creeks and that the hill sides were cleared for gardens and crops to feed their growing herd of cattle and horses. David also wanted to know about hunting prospects. William, being a skilled woodsman, told about the abundance of wild game and fish. All of this pleased David as he was beginning to think ahead about starting his own family when they were established in their new location.

Mary Jane chimed in to ask about their nearest neighbors. William told about a family by the name of Fleming who had passed through their area from Powell Valley and moving into Kentucky. They had settled about a day's trip across the mountain and he had visited them on a couple of occasions. He also told about a family by the name of Potter who had moved into the area of the Breaks which was about twenty miles east. This was good news for Mary Jane to know that there were at least neighbors that could be reached in a day or two.

John asked James if he had been back to the place they had hunted and explored which lay about twelve miles east and downstream from the headwaters of the Pound River. He described it as located about equal distance between two rivers and on a full rushing stream. It had hills rising up from the south and southwest but opened to the west. Also, there was a lush valley with lots of pea vines which would be ideal for grazing livestock.

James said he had. In fact, a lone hunter by the name of William Broadwater had built a small, one room cabin as a winter refuge but had abandoned it about a year ago. As far as he knew, it had not been occupied since.

This was the place John had remembered and thought about many times in the intervening years. He recalled that it was in a remote area and between the two main traveled trails to Kentucky....the one crossing the headwaters of the Pound River leading across the mountain and the other from the Clinch River leading through the Breaks. It was good news that no one had claimed the area and John immediately set his sights on this as his final destination.

After about an hour, realizing it was already early afternoon and they had to make up some lost time, John said they needed to get moving. He thanked James for the information and told him where he was headed to establish his new home. James agreed it was a good decision.

William shook David's hand and said he was looking forward to seeing more of him when they were settled.

James and William gave them a briefing on the trail ahead and suggested they try to make their first camp at the confluence of Roaring Creek and Toe River, which was about eight miles upstream. With that, they waved goodbye and moved on down the trail toward Spruce Pine.

Chapter Five

A Good Day's Journey

David was more eager than ever to get started again after William had shared his experiences. He took the reins of the team of horses and began immediately picking up the pace as they moved out.

John was thinking to himself about the campsite just up the river that James had recommended and remembered it well. It was at a ford that was suitable for the animals and drays to cross even with the spring rains and swollen creek. In fact, he had camped there while passing through on the hunting and exploring trip in 1810. He also recalled the rather flat area on the other side of the creek which would make for good camping. But most of all his mind was occupied with the peaceful little valley that was now his destination to satisfy his hopes and dreams.

The troop pushed steadily onward, maneuvering around hillsides and crossing several small creeks, still following the wagon road up the river. They took only brief rest stops for the animals until they reached Roaring Creek. They were all pleased to have arrived at their destination without incident on the first day out. John estimated they had covered about 20 miles in all.

As evening began to approach, David and Isaac took care of the cattle and hogs by leading them to the creek for water. They built a corral out of large tree limbs and enclosed it with the drays. They could graze on the rich green grass that had emerged from its winter sleep within the corral.

John cared for the horses and tied them with a long

lead rope several yards away so they, too, could graze and rest for the night. In the meantime, Mary Jane was occupied with preparing the evening meal. When it was ready, she called them to supper. They washed up in the creek, gathered around the campfire, sat on rocks and logs, and prepared to enjoy their first meal on the trail. John offered up the blessing as usual. Then their conversation turned to the day's travel and the good food Mary Jane had prepared which included left over ham and fried apple biscuits. After finishing the meal, they checked the animals to make sure they were secured for the night while Mary Jane cleaned up the cooking and eating utensils. With their chores done, they gathered around the campfire to discuss plans for tomorrow's trip.

The sun continued its westward journey and daylight faded into darkness as the pioneer family prepared their bedrolls made of deerskins with quilts tucked inside. It had been a good first day on the trail.

Chapter Six

Close Encounter

John was awakened by the horses moving about restlessly and snorting. He continued to lay quietly and listened to try to determine what was causing them to act that way. When they became more restless, he decided to slip out of his bedroll to investigate.

It was a clear night with the crescent moon providing some visibility to the hollow surrounding Roaring Creek. A light frost was on the grass since they were nearing the halfway point up the mountain. John went immediately to the horses to calm them and noticed that they were all looking toward the creek near the campfire site. From their reaction, he knew something was there but couldn't see what it was. By this time the hounds had joined him but were not eager to give chase to whatever was down there.

He made his way back to David, shook him and whispered for him to get up because he suspected they had an unwanted visitor in camp. As David got out of his bedroll, John eased over to get his rifle without waking Mary Jane or Isaac and retreated toward the horses. David, sensing his father's concern, followed with his rifle. When they got to the horses, John again saw that they were still nervously looking to the area of the campfire and pointed David in that direction. He motioned that he was going to investigate and David should follow a few paces back.

As they crept closer to the dying embers of the fire, John could barely make out the image of a large animal in the dark shadow near the creek. He slowly and cautiously edged his way forward, straining to determine what it was and what it was doing there. Suddenly it stood upright and let out a loud grunt. Immediately he recognized it was a huge black bear and yelled for David to take cover. John raised his rifle and fired a shot aimed well over the bear's head. He instinctively knew that most black bears would run from the noise unless it was a rogue or a female protecting her cubs. This time he was right and the bear fled across the creek and up the hillside. With all of this commotion, the hounds gave chase across the creek for a short distance before returning at the beckoning call of their master.

Mary Jane and Isaac came tearing out of their bedrolls frightened by the yelling and burst of gun fire. John hollered out to them that everything was alright. David was still on full alert just in case the bear decided to return.

Now that they were all awake and being reassured that they were probably safe from the bear, John stirred the coals and threw a few sticks of dried wood on it to build a fire. Mary Jane and Isaac grabbed their coats and quickly moved toward the blazing fire to warm up from the frosty chill in the early morning air.

It wasn't long before a faint daylight was beginning to appear on the eastern horizon and they were now able to move about the campsite. John went to check on the horses and animals in the corral and found them still aroused but secured. While making the round, he wondered what might have attracted the bear so close to camp and went to investigate where he first saw it. He immediately discovered why they had the unwanted visitor. Scraps of food were scattered near the creek from their supper the night before.

"Mary Jane, did you rake out the supper scraps down

here?" John called out.

"Yes, Pa, when I was getting water to heat and wash the supper dishes and pots," she nervously replied because she detected concern in his voice.

"Don't you ever do that again." John admonished her. "That's what the bear was after because they can smell food a long ways off. From now on, be sure all scraps are buried a good distance from camp and our food supplies are secured in the dray."

"Yes, Pa. That won't happen again," she dutifully replied, having learned a valuable lesson on survival in the wilderness.

Now that the camp appeared to be safe and daylight was approaching, John decided it was time to prepare breakfast and get an early start. This would be the day they crossed the mountain and began their descent toward Trade.

Chapter Seven

Up and Over the Blue Ridge

Breakfast was finished. Mary Jane had buried the meal's scraps, cleaned the utensils, stored the food, and secured everything in the dray for the day's journey. Isaac fed and watered the animals. David and John began gearing up the horses and hitching them to the drays. Mary Jane and Isaac doused the campfire with water and covered it with sufficient dirt to smother any remaining embers. They were ready and eager to strike out again.

It was another clear, cold April morning deep in the mountains. The drove of animals, as well as the horses, were a bit frisky and immediately joined the pace set by David. Isaac fell in behind the drove and kept them together and moving easily along. John and Mary Jane took their positions as the little band of determined pioneers headed toward the summit.

After about an hour's steady travel, they rounded a long, sloping curve and the road began to level out and turn westward as it rejoined the Toe River. The stream was getting noticeably smaller, shallower, and only about 30 feet wide. David, however, took note that they were still traveling along the river which meant a continued gradual climb ahead.

In the silence of the cool morning with only the rippling sound of the stream, the muffled noise of the animals and drays, and a few birds whistling softly, David began to imagine what life would be like when he got settled on his new land. The more he thought about it the faster the pace became without him being aware of it. John, however, took note that Mary Jane was beginning to fall back as she led the pack horse and called up to David to slow down. David, being made aware of the faster pace, reigned in the horses to a slower pace.

They had traveled only a short distance further when David called back to his father that he could see smoke coming from a chimney up ahead. The cabin was set back about twenty yards from the road and on the opposite side from the Toe River. As they approached the cabin, a man appeared in the doorway and walked into the enclosed yard to greet them.

"Good morning, friends. Where're you headed, Tennessee or Virginia?" he inquired in a welcoming voice.

"We're on our way to Virginia," David responded.

"Well, you've some way to go and traveling gets rougher after crossing the mountain. Several people have been headed that way lately. They say there's lots of good hunting and some good land to settle on," he offered with a friendly smile, "as for me, this is as far as I'm going. Got me a little land that I can raise my family on and have some livestock right here. Also I meet lots of good folks passing through and get all the news from both ways almost every day from folks coming and going. Seems to me like there's more and more every week."

By the time he finished, Isaac, John, and Mary Jane had moved up and began exchanging greetings. John stepped forward, offered his hand, and introduced himself as John Mullins from Spruce Pine. In exchange, the man introduce himself as Woodrow Houston.

John, being eager to gather all the information he could, asked, "How much further do we have to go before starting down the other side of the mountain?"

"I'd say, it's about an hour or two before you cross over.

Then you'll be going down hill for another couple of hours before coming to where they're mining for ore. That's where you'll be meeting a few folks. From there, they'll let you know which way is the best to go because the road gets a lot rougher for a spell," Mr. Houston responded and then added, "fine looking family you have, Mr. Mullins. Could I offer you all a good breakfast before you move on? I'm sure the wife could muster up enough for a hearty meal."

"Thank you for the offer, Mr. Houston," John graciously replied. "We had an early breakfast and decided to get moving in order to make it well over the mountain today so we can get to Trade around mid day tomorrow. That will be our first rest and resupply stop. So, we best move on to get there on time."

With a firm handshake, Mr. Houston wished them well for their journey and God's blessings for their future.

John gave a nod to David and the little troop began to slowly move on toward the summit.

It wasn't far up the road when they began to see a much larger mountain peak looming in the distance to the east. As the peak came more in view, Mary Jane noticed the leaves on the trees had not begun to show their greenery.

"Pa, what causes the trees at the top of the mountain to be so bare? She asked.

"Well, Mary Jane, the mountain is so tall that frost stays on much longer and the leaves don't come out as early as down below." He paused and then continued, "The mountain had been named Tanawha by the Cherokees who lived and passed through here a long time ago. Then when Daniel Boone opened up the area to folks, they called it Grandfather Mountain 'cause they thought it was like a man's face when they looked up at the top. You'll probably see it when we get over on the other side."

"Okay, I hope so. It's the tallest mountain I've ever seen," she said as she stepped up the pace after having been distracted by peering at the mountain.

David wasn't about to slow down now. He could see a gap that appeared to be the summit and guessed it was only about a half hour ahead. With that he urged the horses on and yelled back to the others to come on.

He was right. They had made it to the top where the road starts down. He pulled the horses over and made room for the others. They came up quickly to take in the scenery of the small valley below.

"As I recollect, it's mostly down hill all the way to Trade from here," John spoke encouragingly. "There's still some rough traveling ahead, especially after we get to where we're going to camp tonight. So, let's get moving."

The road was smoother on the western side because there were more open fields and, too, they were beginning the descent.

They had traveled about an hour when they topped over a knoll and saw small houses built close together just ahead. These were the ore miner's houses. The mines had been in operation several years and had provided lead for the Over Mountain Men on their way to fight the British. As they came closer, they saw small children playing in the yards and waved to them as they passed by.

John remembered when they came to the crossroads that they should take the left fork leading toward Sycamore Shoals, Tennessee for a short distance and then turn due west again. It would take them through the small village of Banner Elk and then on a steep and winding road. Also, it would be a shorter route and take less time to reach their next camp site.

Several people came out to greet them as they continued on the muddy road through Banner Elk. They paused occasionally to exchange brief conversations and gather whatever information they could about the travel conditions that lay ahead. It was also reassuring to Mary Jane and Isaac to speak with several children their ages who eagerly greeted them and inquired about their destination. They even wanted to go with them to the unknown frontier.

The terrain suddenly changed as they made their way out of Banner Elk. The road quickly became steeper. It was rougher, too, having only been smoothed by other pioneers making the same trek. The real challenge for David was to keep a tight rein on the horses and, at the same time, manage the hand brake on the dray to keep it from running into the horses and causing them to bolt. In either case, it could create a major interruption to their plans plus irreparable damage to the dray and all equipment on board. The dray, being a short-wheeled based wagon, was easier to manage in this rough terrain than the traditional longer wagon. It would also prove helpful as the roads ahead turned from Indian trails to mere buffalo traces before reaching their final destination.

David, however, being a stout young man and experienced teamster, held the team in check as they descended the steep and winding trail. Also, Isaac had no problem tending the drove and keeping them moving because the road was very narrow. John was carefully following with the smaller dray and keeping a close eye on Mary Jane. She was tired from the long's day journey and mounted her horse to ride through the rough terrain.

Without mishap they finally made the descent to a beautiful valley tucked between surrounding mountains and flush with streams and farms that had been settled in the late 1790's by the David Hicks and Joseph Mast families. This was the same Watauga River valley which Daniel Boone had traversed in 1767 in search of a suitable route to the western frontier. They found a good campsite along the stream and set up camp for the night. It had been an arduous trip and long day but John was pleased with their progress. This is about where he thought they would be at the end of the second day and in good position to make it to Trade the next day. *(This area would soon come to be known by its present name, Valle Crucis, which is Latin for "Valley of the Cross.)*

Chapter Eight

Trade

With breakfast finished and sunrise approaching, they prepared to break camp and set out with a bit more excitement in hopes of reaching Trade by noon.

They traveled the narrow trail about two hours until they came to a crossroads and entered a more traveled road. It was an established road that came from Boone, North Carolina and used by the ever increasing hunters, traders, land speculators, and pioneers who were moving westward. By 1829, it had become known as *The Daniel Boone Trail* because he had used it in 1767 and subsequent trips to explore this frontier and beyond.

As the sun rose higher over the eastern mountain bringing its warmth to the cool spring morning, their pace quickened. Travel was easier than the daybefore. They only made brief stops to rest and eat the snacks Mary Jane had prepared for the day. The animals were still in good shape as were the drays.

They were beginning to pass more travelers heading back to Boone and even to the Carolinas for various and sundry reasons. The travelers were usually in pairs or small groups and were inquisitive as to their destination. Conversations were brief and often about the time and distance to Trade. Some even took time to tell them about the bustling village and what to expect upon arrival. They were getting closer with each encounter and, without realizing it, they were increasing the pace.

John began going over their supply needs for the remainder of the trip and what to purchase to sustain them until he could return for more essentials to carry them through the next winter. He was not concerned about farm and garden seeds because Ollie had made sure these were included in their preparations before leaving. She had included corn and green beans of different varieties, tomatoes, lettuce, mustard, onions, potatoes, turnips, squash, and pumpkins.

David, on the other hand, was more interested in meeting and talking with the young men and women to find out all he could about their life on the frontier. Also, he was thinking about his future and what he might expect as the migration was pushing further into Kentucky and even Ohio.

Mary Jane was reminiscing about what her mother had said about her responsibilities and about what she needed for the remainder of the trip. She had to plan ahead until they could grow their own vegetables. Therefore, she was busy making a mental list of these supplies and hoped to get them in Trade.

Isaac was a typical 12 year old who just wanted to safely and securely corral his drove and have the opportunity to explore the village.

They were each engrossed in their own thoughts when suddenly David hollered out, "That must be Trade up ahead. It's about a half mile down, on the right."

"I can see people moving about and going from building to building," he called out again.

Their gait increased with this news and every turn of the wheel brought them closer so the others could see the activity. It was an exciting scene to see all the people bustling about the village.

David guided his team into the large open grounds and the others followed until they came to a halt in a space that could easily accommodate their needs.

John quickly moved his dray into position to corral the drove and instructed the others to help Isaac secure the animals. When this was done he told them to water and tie up their horses and then gather up by his dray.

Several small groups were scattered about the grounds swapping news, sharing stories, and enjoying an occasional hearty laugh. It all seemed harmless to the children.

David, Mary Jane, and Isaac finished their tasks and assembled as instructed. Their anticipation of what lay ahead was beginning to build. However, John recalled the rowdiness of some of Trade's clientele from his earlier visit and stories he had heard from travelers passing through Spruce Pine. He immediately took charge and changed their plans.

Trade was commonly known as *The Trading Grounds* and used by the Indians as a bartering site long before Daniel Boone. As more hunters and settlers were passing through, it became a convenient place for merchants to set up businesses. John knew it was a meeting place for wagons coming in and out of Virginia, Tennessee, and the Carolinas hauling apples, tobacco, rifles, knives, skins, corn liquor, and other supplies for the growing population. It was also widely known for men who had too much liquor to drink, fighting, knifing, and even shootings. Therefore, Trade was just a place for them to resupply, stay safe, and quickly move on.

John instructed the boys to stay with their belongings while he and Mary Jane visited the country store to purchase their needs. He warned them to stay alert for certain people who might be on the prowl to steal their property and animals or just to cause trouble. This news came as a surprise to the children as they had not experienced this kind of behavior in their safe community back home.

When John and Mary Jane entered the store, he went directly to the clerk to let him know they wanted to purchase enough supplies to sustain them in the frontier until he could return for the rest of his family in Spruce Pine. The clerk showed him a space to gather their items until they finished shopping. They then went about their shopping and placed their purchases there.

The store was busy with several local shoppers and a few, like them, making large purchases. When they finished shopping John asked the clerk to tally up their purchases and he paid in cash with the newly minted U. S. currency of the day. Mary Jane was sent to take what she could carry and send David back to help with the remainder. Meanwhile, the clerk provided John a large two-wheeled cart to carry their supplies to the drays.

With their supplies secured on the drays, John was eager to get started. He didn't want to risk his family seeing or being involved in any unsavory activities in Trade. He told his children to prepare to leave immediately in order to find a suitable camping spot well out of Trade before dark. Once again the children were disappointed but accepted their father's decision.

They had only spent about two hours in Trade when they moved out of *The Trading Grounds* onto *The Daniel Boone Trail*, continuing as before on a gradual descent down the mountain.

Because they were refreshed and had a smooth road, it took only about four hours to travel the next ten miles to Shouns Crossroads where the roads split again. Shouns Crossroads had been established by Leonard and Barbara Shouns in 1792 as a trading post. Mr. Shouns hauled merchandise and supplies from Baltimore, Maryland down the Shenandoah Valley to Abingdon, Virginia and up the mountain to his trading post. *(Shouns Crossroads later became Taylorsville and eventually Mountain City.)*

The Mullins family took the road used by Shouns' supply wagons. The other road went south into Tennessee. As the sun was approaching the western horizon they located a good camping site on Cold Springs Creek just beyond the intersection and set up camp.

John took note that before the sun went down it faded behind heavy dark clouds. He knew that if the clouds kept coming from that direction they could get a rain before tomorrow's daybreak. But since they were still high on the mountain and the clouds a long way off, it was difficult to predict which direction they would take. He made no mention of this to his children and soon they were tucked in for the night.

Chapter Nine

Appalachian Spring

At first it was a low rolling sound that woke John. He laid quietly and listened to determine if it were approaching them. It didn't take long to realize the rumble was getting louder and this could be one of the fast moving storms that frequently occurred in these mountains. Quietly getting dressed, he saw the flashes of lightning and heavy storms clouds approaching and they were directly in the storm's path. The sound of thunder was also getting louder.

John estimated it was a couple of hours before daylight and the storm would probably reach them before it became light enough to prepare breakfast, pack up, and move out. His experience with the spring rains had taught him that it would be better to keep moving rather than staying put. A storm like this was usually very cold, even with sleet or hail, and could be a downpour. Knowing that they would be crossing several streams, which could overflow their banks and block their progress, he called the children to get up and prepare to move out without breakfast. He hoped the storm would pass quickly and, if so, they would stop and eat.

By the time they were packed and ready to leave, the rain started. At first it began sprinkling and slowly increased to a steady rain. Thunder and lightning became louder and more severe. Then suddenly the rain came in a down pour. The road turned to mud as streams of water flowed down its path. Their clothes quickly became soaked yet they continued as fast as they could under the conditions. However, they were moving and John felt safer from the severe lightning than huddled together in camp.

The rain did not let up but they kept going. Cold Spring Creek was beginning to rise and, in places, overflow its banks. They even waded through several overflowing small streams. Then Cold Spring Creek emptied into the larger Furnace Creek but still within its banks. They kept driving on until it became full daylight. Within an hour the thunder and lightning appeared to be moving ahead of them. They all, and particularly John, felt a sense of relief, hoping that the worst of the rain was passing. It wasn't long until the rain began to ease up. With this, John decided to take a brief stop to check on his children and animals. He hollered for David to find a place to pull over. He found a rise in the road where they would not be standing in water and pulled over.

Immediately John directed everyone to make a quick check on the animals and then assemble at his dray. As each arrived, he inquired about their conditions and whether they were able to continue on until the rain ceased. Mary Jane was quick to let him know that her clothes were soaked and she was very cold. Isaac and David gave the same response but said they were willing to keep moving because they didn't think it would get any better until the rain stopped. They all agreed.

John said he expected the rain to pass shortly and it wasn't far until they would arrive at Laurel Bloomery where an iron ore forge mill was being constructed when he passed through the area in 1810. Also, by then the rain should stop and the mill might provide them a place to get inside to change into dry clothes and prepare something to eat.

So, once again, they began sloshing down the muddy road. The dark clouds soon began to give way and the rain slowed to a drizzle. This lifted their spirits and increased the pace until they came in sight of the mill. By the time they reached it and parked along side a swollen Furnace Creek, the rain had stopped.

Joseph Gentry, the owner, saw them coming and went out on the porch to welcome and invite them into the forge. As each one secured their charges and entered, he presented a cup of hot cider kept on the pot-bellied stove in the center of the large mill room. After the usual introductions and inquiry, he directed them to a spare room where they could change into some dry clothes.

Mary Jane changed first because she was beginning to shiver. When she came out Mr. Gentry greeted her with another cup of cider and invited her to prepare their meal on the stove and eat inside. She graciously accepted and hastily went to the dray to gather the necessary items to prepare a late breakfast.

Following their meal and enjoying good conversations with Mr. Gentry, John informed his children that they must get going to make it to the village of Damascus before nightfall. Mr. Gentry assured them that Furnace Creek would not be out of its banks and they could easily be in Damascus within three to four hours.

They all thanked Mr. Gentry for his hospitality and stepped out into the bright sunshine and fresh air left by the Appalachian spring rain.

The road was still muddy and Furnace Creek full but within its banks when they took their usual formation and slowly pulled away, waving good-bye to Mr. Gentry.

Travel was not as difficult as earlier today and, once they were moving, David set a steady pace that was comfortable for his family. John was pleased they broke camp when they did this morning and survived the storm without mishap. He was confident now that they would reach their next destination in plenty of time to set up camp and prepare for the evening.

It was only a short distance until the road became more narrow. It meandered in a winding descent between Furnace Creek and the steep hillsides and cliffs. They had traveled about an hour when they took note of a survey marker identifying the state lines separating Virginia and Tennessee. Then they crossed a recently constructed bridge below the confluence of Furnace Creek and Beaver Dam Creek. Shortly after crossing the bridge, they reached the small village of Damascus well before sunset and chose a level site to camp along the South Fork of the Holston River.

John was surprised at the increased population of Damascus and stores since he last passed through it. Also, while setting up camp, feeding and securing the animals, several residents stopped by to exchange information and offer helpful travel suggestions. During these conversations David and Isaac learned of the abundant fish in the river and how to catch them. When their chores were finished, they rushed off to try their hand at catching enough for supper. They returned in time for Mary Jane to add fish to her menu.

Following supper, they sat down around the campfire to talk about what lay ahead now that they were off the mountain. John explained that travel for the next two to three days would be easier because this part of Virginia had been settled for several years and roads had improved as settlers were pushing further west. He concluded their discussion with his vision of what was waiting for them at the end of their journey. Meanwhile Mary Jane felt chilled from the soaking she took during the morning storm.

With the pleasant sounds of the rushing South Fork of the Holston River and the repetitive song of the whip-poor-will, they retired for the night.

Chapter Ten

A Pioneer's Illness

Morning arrived with the crispness of a clear April day in the foothills of the magnificent Appalachian mountains. Mocking birds were out as usual just before daybreak singing their clarion songs welcoming a new day and woke the Mullins family. There was a renewed excitement in camp to get started. Each of the men tended to his chores while Mary Jane prepared another sumptuous breakfast. By the time they had eaten and made preparations to move out, Damascus was beginning to come alive with its residents and travelers stirring about town.

Just as the sun was appearing over the crest of the ridge behind them, the troop headed down a well traveled road determined to reach Abingdon by noon.

Since leaving their home in Spruce Pine four days ago they had traveled through North Carolina and Tennessee, which had been admitted as the sixteenth state of the United States in 1796. They were now in Washington County, Virginia, which was formed in 1776 by the Virginia General Assembly. It was the first locality named for President George Washington.

Ease of travel was a pleasant surprise for John since the road was now a major supply link between the Great Valley of Virginia by way of The Wilderness Road and the Carolinas. Individuals who were traveling on business or visiting relatives could now choose a stage coach service for their journeys. Taking notice of this progress, John was urged on toward his ultimate destination for concern that someone would beat him to it and make a claim before he arrived.

Within a couple of hours they had already crossed the swollen South Fork of the Holston River and the Middle Fork of the Holston River and should be in Abingdon by noon. Realizing this, John began to set his sight on reaching the North Fork of the Holston River before sunset. Still feeling flush with a chill, Mary Jane continued without telling anyone.

Daniel Boone and his partner, Nathaniel Gist, first visited the area in 1760. They camped at what they called "Wolf Hills" because a pack of wolves attacked at night and killed some of their dogs. Then, in 1774, Joseph Black erected a fort nearby and named it "Black's Fort". It remained as Black's Fort and became Washington County's seat of government in 1776 until the name changed again when Abingdon was incorporated in 1778. The name Abingdon was adopted for Martha Washington's English home, Abingdon Parish.

By 1829, the town had a population of several hundred people. It had become an important intersection for travel and commerce from the Great Valley of Virginia to the Carolinas, Tennessee, and further into the rich valleys of Southwestern Virginia and Kentucky.

The Mullins family entered Abingdon from the east. As they approached the center of town they passed *The Tavern*, a popular eating and gathering place for locals and visitors to discuss the affairs of the day. The stately courthouse at the top of hill came into view and was the largest and most impressive building they had seen. Saddled horses and small carriages were tied to hitching posts along the wide street. People were busy conducting their daily chores and businesses. Supply wagons, small bands of settlers with their droves of animals, travelers on horseback, and carriages created a steady stream moving in both directions.

They made their way past the courthouse to the west end of town. When they came to an intersection that John recognized, he called for a rest break. It was a militia gathering place known as *The Mustering Ground* where in September, 1780, four hundred men under the command of General William Campbell began their march to Fort Watauga at Sycamore Shoals, Tennessee. There they joined other frontier fighters and continued their march to King's Mountain where they defeated the British in a decisive turning point of the Revolutionary War.

The Mustering Ground was now used as a convenient place for settlers to stop for a rest, check wagons, animals, and supplies before launching forth into the rapidly expanding frontier.

Mary Jane especially welcomed the stop. She was now feeling a fever coming on and it seemed to be getting worse with each passing hour. She did not want to tell anyone because it might delay them to care for her. Instead, she continued preparing a meal as if nothing was wrong.

Meanwhile, John and David helped Isaac corral his drove and then went to tend to their horses and check the drays to get ready to move on after a short rest and something to eat.

When the men had completed their checks, fed the animals, and washed in a nearby stream, they returned to find Mary Jane had prepared a light meal of dried jerky and blackberry jam with biscuits left over from breakfast.

John first took note that she was nibbling on her's and sitting very quietly.

He continued taking short glances at her and then asked, "Mary Jane are you feeling alright?"

She looked up with a weak smile, "Yes, Pa. I guess I'm just a bit tired and chilled. But, I'll be feeling better when we make camp and can get a good night's sleep."

"Well, you don't look good to me," John said, "but I'll keep a close eye on you and if you get any worse off, you let me know before you take a fever. We can't afford to let you get sick."

"Okay, Pa. I'll be sure to let you know."

"Now, let's finish eating so we can get going right away. We don't have but a short distance to the North Fork of the Holston River where we may have trouble crossing because of the rain yesterday," John stood up as he spoke.

From *The Mustering Ground*, they headed almost due north. The road was well traveled since Russell County had been formed in 1786 and small communities were beginning to spring up with more settlers coming to the area to buy cheap land to farm and raise their families.

As they moved further away from Abingdon, the road began a slight downgrade, which, coupled with a smooth road, made their travel easier. John kept looking back to check on Mary Jane. After about an hour, he saw her pull the horse over to a large boulder and mount up to ride. He slowed down to wait for her to catch up.

"How' you feeling, Mary Jane?" he asked when she came along side his dray.

"I think I'm getting a fever, Pa. But let's keep moving because you said we should be down to the Holston River in a short while. I think I can make it there."

"Yeah, we should be there in less than two hours. If you can make it, we'll stop by the river for the night."

She wrapped herself with another coat for added warmth and urged her horse to keep pace with the rest. When they started down a steep descent and rounded sharper curves, she knew they were about to reach the river.

As soon as John saw the river, he hollered up for David to cross the bridge and find a site for them to spend the night. He was concerned that Mary Jane might be getting the grippe.

They pulled off the road into an area that had been used frequently for camping by the many travelers and settlers who had gone before them.

"David, you and Isaac corral the drove, secure the horses and take care of Mary Jane's horse. I have to look after her."

He helped her down from the horse and felt her shivering body and high fever. He knew she was seriously ill and that he had to do something quickly to break the fever. He leaned her against a tree. Then he grabbed her bedroll with an extra quilt and placed them in a protected area. He ran to his dray to get the gallon of homemade liquor he brought along for medicinal purposes.

"Isaac, get a fire going for a pot of boiling water to make a toddy."

John went back to his dray to get some honey, ginger, and sassafras to mix with the liquor and hot water to make the toddy. He knew, since it was the only medicine available, this was the quickest way to break a fever.

As soon as Isaac had the water boiling, John poured a half cup of water in the mixture and held Mary Jane as she sipped the toddy. After she had taken a few sips, he helped her to the bedroll and tightly tucked in the covers to keep her warm. Then he gave her a few more sips before she fell asleep.

John and his sons moved quietly about preparing camp and fixing their meal. As night began to fall, they checked the animals and made plans to turn in before dark.

"You boys join me around the fire to pray for Mary Jane's healing," he softly spoke in a worried tone to his boys.

When they finished praying, John got up without speaking and quietly placed his bedroll beside hers should she wake up in the night and need him. Then he crawled in and lay awake listening to her rhythmic breathing and before long he was asleep.

Mary Jane slept through the night and when she awoke she started rustling to get out of the bedroll.

"Mary Jane, don't get uncovered just yet," John warned her.

"How are you feeling?" he asked.

"I'm much better and I believe the fever is gone. But my bedroll is wet with sweat."

"That's a good sign. You stay put until I can get a fire going and another quilt to wrap you in so you won't get chilled all over again."

"David. Isaac. Get up and take care of the animals. Mary Jane is feeling better and, if she's able to travel, we'll get going before long," John called out with relief in his voice.

He quickly stoked the fire with several large pieces of wood. After it caught up enough, he got another quilt for her to wrap in and get near the fire to keep warm.

"Mary Jane, when you feel like it, you can get into some dry clothes. Just make sure you stay warm," John told her as he began to prepare breakfast.

After breakfast was over, Mary Jane assured her father that the fever was gone and she felt well enough to travel. However, she may have to ride her horse for a while because she felt too weak to walk.

This was good news for the family because a high fever left untreated could have become deadly for Mary Jane. And, too, because she had recovered so quickly, they could soon be on the move, without further delay.

Preparations were hastily made to get going as soon as they could break camp and hitch up the drays.

As light fog rose over the North Fork of the Holston River, they pulled out to climb the steep mountain that loomed ahead.

Chapter Eleven

Friendly Pioneer Greeting

Their climb was difficult. The road became narrow and rocky as it wound its way along the mountain side. They stopped frequently to rest the animals and check on Mary Jane's condition. She was still weak from the high fever but able to continue. Due to these conditions, it took more time than expected to reach the top where the road leveled out.

They soon came to another split in the road. One turned due north that would have taken them toward the Kentucky and Ohio territories and the other turned westward. John directed them to take the latter. Before noon they had reached the home and frontier store of Henry and Elizabeth Bickley Dickenson. It was a popular stopping place for travelers going to and from outposts further west.

The Mullins family stopped in front of the large log house to gather as much information as they could about the traveling conditions that lay ahead. Mr. Dickenson first appeared from a nearby building to greet them.

"Good morning, strangers. Glad you stopped to rest a spell," Mr. Dickenson called out.

"Good morning to you, sir," John responded.

"Where're you headed?"

"To a place I hunted some twenty years ago. It's over near Kentucky and about three days trip from here."

"We've seen several families headed in that direction recently. By the way, my name is Henry, Henry Dickenson, and what's yours?"

"John Mullins," he warmly replied while extending his hand, "and this here's my sons, David and Isaac and my daughter, Mary Jane."

"Good morning, sir," they spoke in unison to Mr. Dickenson.

"Where'd you come from?" he asked.

"From Spruce Pine, North Carolina," John replied.

"Well, you've come quite a distance and probably been on the road a few days, haven't you?"

"Yes, sir. This is our sixth day and we may have three to four more to go."

"How about your children? They making the journey alright?"

"Mary Jane had a fever yesterday, but other than being a little weak, she's about over it now."

"So, that's why you're riding, young lady?" Mr. Dickenson directed his question to Mary Jane.

"Yes, sir," she responded.

Mr. Dickenson turned to the house where he saw Elizabeth standing in the door and called to her, "Elizabeth, come here and meet Mary Jane. She's been under the weather and you need to check her temperature before they move on."

David helped Mary Jane dismount while Elizabeth made her way down.

"Tell me what happened to you, young lady?" Elizabeth asked.

"Day before yesterday we traveled through a storm and we all got soaking wet and I got chilled before I could change into dry clothes and get warm. Then last night Pa fixed me a toddy and I slept all night. This morning I felt better," she explained.

"Well, let me feel your forehead, to see if you have any

fever."

As Mrs. Dickenson was feeling her forehead, throat, and back of the neck, Mary Jane could sense the motherly touch and hear it in her soft voice. This brought back memories of her own mother's tender touch and loving care.

Mrs. Dickenson, having completed her examination, informed Mary Jane that she couldn't feel any fever and she should be able to travel providing she rode the horse. She also told John that there was no fever and that he should prepare another toddy for her tonight just to take care of any remaining symptoms.

While Mrs. Dickenson was taking care of Mary Jane, the boys were busy checking the animals and keeping the drove together and John was asking Henry about the travel conditions and distances to the next settlements. Henry, being a man of means and well respected by his neighbors, informed John that travel to a small village on the Clinch River was less than twenty miles away by a road that he had constructed for the State of Virginia in 1792. It was a good road that should allow them to arrive there before sunset.

John gathered his family and told them to prepare to leave. Mary Jane thanked Mrs. Dickenson with a hug and mounted her horse to wait her father's directions. David and Isaac made preparations and they, too, looked to their father to give the word to move out. John shook Henry's hand and thanked him and Mrs. Dickenson for their hospitality. Then he nodded to David to lead the way. Mary Jane glanced back and waved to Mr. and Mrs. Dickenson as they departed.

Their travel to Clinch River was as Mr. Dickenson had described to John and, after crossing the river at Gist's

Ford, they came to a small frontier settlement. Although the sun had passed behind the western horizon when they arrived, John was pleased to inform his children that they should reach their final destination in no more than three days.

Mary Jane was very tired because of her recent bout with the fever and the long day's journey but she made no complaint and began to prepare the evening meal. John and his boys tended to their chores and prepared camp for the night.

Following their supper and the usual conversation about the day's journey, they took their bedrolls and placed them around the campfire. Then Mary Jane reminded her father to prepare the toddy to make sure the fever didn't come back. After taking a few sips of the toddy, she crawled into her bedroll and was soon asleep. John was the last to retire. He lay awake for some time thinking about what lay ahead for him and his family since they were now, literally, on the fringe of western civilization.

(Part of this house was first built on the north side of the Clinch River in 1769 by Henry and Elizabeth Dickenson. The original logs of the Dickenson house were combined with the original logs of the Thomas Bundy house to restore the Dickenson-Bundy Log House in 1975 on its present site in Dickensonville, VA. Russell County had been established on January 2, 1786 from a section of Washington County and the first court held in the home of William Robinson at Castlewood on May 1, 1786. Also, the Dickensons built the second Russell County Courthouse of stone in 1799 in Dickensonville. It served as the courthouse until 1818 when Lebanon became the county seat. The author recommends a visit to these well preserved buildings, filled with period furnishings, to experience what it was like to live in the late 1700 and early 1800's.)

Chapter Twelve

The Western Frontier Border

Political squabbles, heated debates, and divisive elections were taking place along the eastern seaboard, especially in the ever increasing large cities, throughout the 1820's and beyond. The main issues were: how to grow the economy; slavery, which split the industrial northern and agrarian southern states; and the expansion of the vast western territory. However, these issues were of little concern to the pioneers who were far removed by distance and communications and had issues of a different kind. Their primary concerns centered around moving further away from such chaos and acquiring land on which to provide for their families and live in peace. They were a very independent and self-sufficient people who had made their escape from imperial governments in their homelands. They wanted nothing to do with this kind of government now that they had found the freedom they were seeking. This became the driving force for them and the reason so many were willing to risk their lives, families, meager belongings, and extreme hardships to pursue their dreams. It was the life John wanted for his family more than anything else.

The next morning, and for the first time since leaving Spruce Pine, John began to take note of the small frontier settlement where he now camped. Cabins were scattered about with a good distance between them. Land around the cabins had been cleared for farming and more was being cleared for spring planting. Freshly plowed gardens were already planted near the cabins. Children were playing in the fields, woods, and along the Clinch River. Even some of the older children were fishing to help supply food for their tables. Adults were hard at work improving their homestead. All sorts of activities were happening everywhere he looked. This was the kind of settlement he envisioned for himself and his family when his children were married and had their own families.

Before they broke camp, John again sought out another local person to gather as much information as he could about the settlement and what lay ahead of them for the day's journey. He approached a man plowing a nearby field and learned that his settlement had been established in 1790 by Peter Francis de Tubeuf, a Frenchman and his relatives, who came to America to escape the French Revolution. It was first called Ste. Marie French Settlement but was short lived because Mr. de Tubeuf was murdered by robbers in 1795 and then abandoned by his heirs shortly thereafter. As other settlers moved in, it grew and the name was changed to St. Paul. Additionally, John learned that the settlement was in Russell County which now extended to the Kentucky border. The farmer also told him that small bands of Indians were still using it as a hunting ground. For the most part, raids on settlements were practically unknown because the Governor of Virginia had established several forts throughout the region to protect its settlers. Their conversation ended when the farmer volunteered that the nearest "sign of life" was known as Guest Station, which only had a few settlers widely scattered about the surrounding area. It was about twelve to fourteen miles further west but the road was rough and would take most of the day to make the trip with their drays and animals.

John retreated to the camp with this information and instructed his children to make haste to get started because he expected travel to be the roughest they had experienced thus far. He said it probably would be more like they had experienced from Banner Elk to Valle Crucis on the second day of their trip, only further.

They were quickly on their way and within a short distance they began climbing a steep hill where the road narrowed to just a wagon trail. No sooner had they climbed the hill when the trail started down a steep descent. It was a difficult and tiring trip, not only for the family but also for the animals. Furthermore, throughout the entire day they did not see a single cabin or sign of land being cleared by settlers. Instead, the terrain was very hilly and the trail closely followed small streams and hollows. This was typical of the day's journey all the way to Guest Station *(Coeburn)*.

They arrived at Guest Station before dark. John remembered it well as a frontier outpost or station for settlers, travelers, and hunters to take refuge during Indian raids. Several pioneer homesteads were scattered along the river and nearby the station that were not there when he passed through before. Also, the station itself had some small cabins bunched together, as if for protection, and even a few shelters and lean-tos more suitable for hunters and trappers than pioneers. After crossing a creek and not wanting to camp near the station, John took the lead and turned due north away from the road that led to Powell Valley and Kentucky. They continued another mile or so before he chose a large, level bottom to set up camp several yards from the trail.

The family had just settled around the campfire at dusk for their usual evening routine when they heard voices coming from the direction they would be traveling tomorrow. At first the voices were muffled, but within minutes they were louder and more distinct. Silence fell around the fire. Then, as the voices came closer, they saw four raucous men coming down the path leading horses. Tensions increased around the campfire and with each approaching step, it became obvious the men were "liquored up".

John secured his rifle by his side and told David to stay put with his rifle ready. Then, in a hushed but tense tone, he commanded Mary Jane and Isaac to take cover in his dray, each with a rifle, and not make any noise.

As the men approached, John recognized that they were returning from a winter hunt with furs packed on poles and tied to their horses, Indian style. It was likely they were coming back to trade or sell their valuable hides. Since it was not uncommon for men who had spent long winter months in the wilds to imbibe in the spirits to celebrate their success, he also knew they could sometimes "get out of hand". Therefore, his immediate concern was for the safety of his family.

John and David remained seated by the campfire as the men passed about thirty yards away. They gave a friendly wave to the passers-by but did not get up to greet or give them cause to stop.

The hunters waved back and gave a few shouts of profanity. Two even waved their whiskey bottles to invite John and David to share a drink. The offer was politely waved off and the hunters continued without incident. John waited until they were out of sight and sound before calling Mary Jane and Isaac to rejoin them around the fire.

This was another valuable lesson on survival in the wilderness for the children, especially Mary Jane.

Chapter Thirteen

An Unexpected Challenge

The next morning they awoke early, excited about the promise of reaching their final destination today. It being their eighth day of travel, the morning chores were routine and each one pitched in to prepare to leave as soon as possible. In fact, they weren't even aware of the light frost that covered the surrounding area.

Within an hour, they were on their way following the trail the hunters used last evening. Travel was easy as they meandered along the creek. More than likely it had been used by the Cherokee and Shawnee Indians as a War Path when fighting over these rich hunting grounds. They saw evidence of farming in the bottom land and some homesteads were set back near the foothills. But this time John knew where he was and didn't stop for information because he remembered returning to North Carolina on the same trail years ago.

Before long, the trail turned up a mountain side with just enough width for the drays. Travel became more challenging than anything they had faced before. David, managing his team of horses and larger dray, moved at a much slower pace. At times he had to walk beside the horses to keep from stepping off the steep hillside. He stopped several times during the climb to let his horses rest. When he reached the top, he pulled over for the others to come along side to take a well deserved break, not only for the animals but also for him and his family.

Except for the descent down the other side of the rugged mountain, their travel continued without delay until they came to a swift flowing stream and followed it for quite a distance. John recalled that this stream flowed into a river where he and his brothers had seen hundreds of whooping cranes. They were so impressed by the numbers that they called it the "Cranesnest River."

It was about noon, with bright sunshine making their travel more pleasant, when David suddenly yelled out that the trail ahead was blocked by trees that were uprooted and across the trail. The trees had new leaves on the branches and fresh dirt still on their roots. Therefore, it was clear that a recent storm had passed that way.

John immediately took charge and began telling his children what to do. The first thing he needed was to find out how far it was blocked and how much they would have to remove to make it through.

"David, tie up your team and go see how far the trail is blocked and what we have to do to clear it," was his first directive.

"Mary Jane, you help Isaac pen up the animals. It may take us a while to clear this."

"I'll get out the axes and saws and get started. When David gets back we'll know how much we have to cut through before we can get going again."

David started making his way through the thick mountain laurel by going around the large trees and thick brush rather than crawling over, under, or through them.

Mary Jane and Isaac penned up the animals with a make-shift corral of limbs, brush, and the drays and carried water to them from the nearby creek.

John grabbed his axe and began chopping the brush so they could get to the larger trees when David returned.

After taking care of their assignments, Mary Jane and Isaac joined in by removing the cuttings and piling them off the trail.

When David was close enough, he hollered out enthusiastically as he thrashed through the thick laurels, "It's blocked about a hundred yards or so and then there's only small stuff on the trail all the way to the river."

"You all sure have cleared out a bunch," he continued, out of breath, as he grabbed an axe and joined in. "I believe we can cut our way through, but it's going to take a few hours."

"As you can see, I'm a bit ahead of Mary Jane and Isaac," John said in between swings. "When we finish clearing the brush, we'll get the crosscut saw and start on the bigger trees. Then we'll hitch up the horses and move the logs off the trail so we can get the drays through."

John and David finished cutting their way through the brush and returned to use the two-man crosscut to saw the trees into logs that would be easy to move.

Mary Jane and Isaac continued piling the brush until they had it cleared. Then they returned to get the next assignment from their father.

"Isaac," John said, "you go fetch the chain and log grab from David's dray and unhitch the horses to get ready to move the logs. But, before you do that, bring us a good cool drink from the spring on the hillside over there."

"Mary Jane, while he's doing that, you can fix us something to eat. We'll all be hungry by the time we finish cutting these trees."

They were miles from Guest Station and the nearest settler. But, it was not a feeling of being alone because they had each other. This interdependence created a strong sense of togetherness and willingness to do whatever it took to achieve the interconnected dream they now shared. Therefore, they did their jobs willingly and then looked around to see what else needed to be done. The scene was like a family of beavers working tirelessly to complete their lodge.

In all, it took over four hours to cut and move the brush, saw the trees, and clear the logs so the drays could get through. And, by the time they finished, it was late in the afternoon and not enough time to make it the rest of the way during daylight hours.

John decided to hitch up the drays and move to the Cranesnest River where they would find a more comfortable campsite to spend the night. And, too, they had worked hard to clear the trail and needed the rest to finish their journey tomorrow.

Chapter Fourteen

New Beginnings

    Following a well deserved rest and good night's sleep, they were on the trail at sunrise with expectations of arriving at their destination today. This brought renewed exuberance to the family, as well as, a strong sense of accomplishment. They had survived the arduous journey of the past nine days and now found themselves alone in the wilderness depending on each other for survival. The trip thus far was especially gratifying to Mary Jane who had turned fourteen only a month before and was eager to help establish a new home for her family.

    As they moved along the smooth and sometimes sandy banks of the Cranesnest River, she began to think seriously about her future. She wondered about the remoteness of her new home with the nearest family at least a day's journey by horseback. But then, she was comforted knowing that other families were stretching out in the unknown frontier by way of the Powell Valley road into nearby Kentucky and more were on their way. What she had observed so far were rough and rugged mountains with deep valleys hugging streams and rivers. This was not what she had envisioned from her father's description of a broad, low valley and mountains surrounding on three sides. The more she thought about her future, the deeper she drifted into daydreaming about it. Then suddenly her father called out to David to take a rest before they crossed the stream ahead. This brought her back to reality, but not before she concluded that her father had always made good decisions for the family and this would be no different.

It was only about the ninth hour of a beautiful morning when the little troop forded the stream and began their climb up a narrow trail, leaving the Cranesnest River. It quickly became more like a beaten path than anything they had traveled before. In fact, David became acutely aware of the value of the drays as he made his way upward. They cleared the rocks and boulders easier than the traditional wagon because they were built with a short-wheeled design. His biggest challenge, however, came when the path leaned toward the downside and the dray nearly toppled over. By skillfully maneuvering his team, he was successful in reaching the summit. The others followed without incident.

The path's condition slowed their pace until they finally came to a gap that John had patiently waited to see. It was the entrance to the valley he had thought so much about the last twenty years. A lump swelled in his throat from the emotions of finally arriving at the place of his dream. As they passed through the gap and the valley spread out before them, he called a halt and announced to his children that they had arrived. After they had taken a few minutes to soak in the surroundings, he gathered them together for a prayer of God's blessings on their new land.

Then John took the lead and directed them to a place a short distance down stream where the valley spread out more. He stopped and declared that this was the same spot where he stood twenty years ago and this would be their new home. It just happened to be where the remnants of William Broadwater's cabin still remained. The rushing stream, the abundant pea vine, and the lush valley surrounding them was just as John remembered it. David, Mary Jane, and Isaac stood gazing all around, as if they had seen it before through their father's stories around their hearth back in North Carolina.

"Well, my children, here it is, your new home," John proudly announced, "to me, it may be the most beautiful place on God's green earth."

His children remained speechless while slowly moving about to take in all that was before them. The silence penetrated their being. Not even the animals seemed to be stirring. The beauty of the afternoon sun approaching the horizon and leaving behind its long shadows created a breathless sight to behold.

John took notice of their reactions and waited a brief spell before breaking the silence.

"Mary Jane, what do you think?" he spoke, almost reverently.

"Pa, it's more than anything I ever imagined," she quietly responded.

Then David chimed in, "Pa. Is all this land ours?"

"Yeah, son, it is, but I'll have to execute a contract and apply for a patent at the Russell County Courthouse as soon as I can. The governor of Virginia is encouraging people, like us, to settle the land this far out and he's granting mortgages for a reasonable amount."

After a brief respite, John began issuing instructions to make camp in the one room Broadwater cabin. The real work of clearing, cutting, and building would begin early the next morning.

Chapter Fifteen

Establishing a Wilderness Homestead

They were up at dawn, eager to begin making plans for their cabin, building pens and corrals for the animals, and clearing and plowing the land for gardens and crops. All of this work had to be completed before mid September when John planned to go back to North Carolina to bring the remainder of his family to their new home.

Their immediate tasks were to select a site for their cabin, begin building a place for Mary Jane to prepare their meals, and set up the drays to work out of until they could construct the cabin.

While Mary Jane prepared their usual breakfast, John selected the site a short distance from the creek and the boys tied the horses to long ropes for grazing. The cattle, hogs, and chickens were left to free range. The tall grass and pea vine provided them excellent food.

Following breakfast, John and David grabbed saws and axes and began clearing the cabin site. Mary Jane and Isaac took the scythes and started cutting the grass and pea vine. By noon, they had cleared an area large enough for the cabin, yard, and a garden spot. Then, in the afternoon they gathered rocks to build a chimney. It was John's plan to build the chimney first and then construct the cabin around it so Mary Jane would have a permanent hearth to prepare their meals. As the day came to a close, they sat around the campfire talking about how pleased they were with the location and work they had accomplished.

By the end of May, the chimney was completed and the main room separated from two bedrooms. The cabin began to take shape by late June with the outside walls nearly completed. The gardens were growing well in the fresh, fertile soil and the animals were regaining weight and strength. Sturdier corrals and pens were erected to secure the animals at night. The work was hard and the days long. It was beginning to take its toll since they had been laboring seven days a week from sunrise to sunset.

John noticed that their excitement and energy had waned and progress slowed down. Although he wanted to keep working to be sure the homestead was finished in time to leave for Spruce Pine and return before winter, he recognized that they needed a couple of days to rejuvenate, especially Mary Jane and Isaac. Since the next day would be the Fourth of July, it would be a good time to observe Independence Day and give thanks for their new home and freedom. With the needed rest in mind and to remind his children to always be thankful for their freedom, he declared a two day period of rest. Then he gave strict instructions to do only the necessary chores, rest, take naps, hunt, explore their surroundings on horseback, or whatever they wanted to do. But, there would be no strenuous work on the cabin, in the gardens, or clearing land...just rest and relaxation.

After two days, their young bodies had renewed strength and energy. They were, once again, eager to complete the cabin, clear more land, and plow more fields for corn and wheat to harvest in the fall.

As John and David hewed logs and hoisted them into place, Mary Jane and Isaac prepared the "mud" to fill the cracks and chinks. Once the outside walls were finished, they installed pine flooring, erected inside walls that separated the large main room from two bedrooms, and built a loft. They split chestnut logs into slats for the overlapping roof.

Meanwhile, Mary Jane was busy unloading tables, chairs, and various other household items and filling the kitchen with supplies, utensils, and cookware.

It was late August and the hot summer months were behind them. A touch of fall was in the air when they completed the cabin's interior. Their gardens had produced an abundance of vegetables that now needed their attention. So when time came to start putting up their food supply for the winter, John dug large holes in nearby hillsides and lined the bottoms and sides with heavy straw. They carried turnips, Irish potatoes, and sweet potatoes from the gardens to be snugly placed in the holes and covered with heavy straw and dirt to protect them from freezing during the cold months ahead. They strung green beans with a needle and thread and hung them to dry in the loft. They shelled and dried beans in the sun before putting them in air-tight containers to preserve them. All of these would supply food for their table throughout the winter and be a welcomed addition to their abundant supply of wild game.

David and John pulled ears of corn from the stalks and stored them in a hastily built crib. Then they cut the stalks and made fodder shocks that were left in the field. They used a cradle to cut the wheat and bundled it to retain the kernels for making bread. Then they used mowing blades to cut the hay and let it dry to be put in haystacks. This would supplement the animals' winter grazing.

Life was not easy for these pioneers who were completely isolated from the outside world. The work was hard, the weather was sometimes harsh, and just to survive was a constant challenge. But, they were accustomed to it and, with a steadfast determination and strong faith, they continued to work toward their hopes and dreams.

September was approaching and time for John to make preparations to return for Ollie and the other children. When considering how he would move his family back to Virginia and, at the same time protect his new property, he concluded that David, Mary Jane, and Isaac would stay with the homestead. It was an easy decision since they had proven worthy of his trust and were capable of doing the work to keep it going and protect it until he returned. Then, as he had done when they left Spruce Pine, John assigned duties and responsibilities. David was to keep up the outside work, make ready for winter, and look out for their safety. Mary Jane was in charge of the cabin and its care and Isaac was to take care of the cattle, hogs, and chickens.

At daybreak on a clear, late September morning, John hitched the team of horses to an empty dray and set out for Spruce Pine. David, Mary Jane, and Isaac watched as their father disappeared back into the wilderness. Then they went to work on their morning chores.

Chapter Sixteen

Alone In the Wilderness

It was now October. John had left for North Carolina two weeks earlier and expected to return by mid October. David and Isaac had worked hard to catch up on the farm chores and Mary Jane had put things in order in the cabin. They were pleased with the work they had accomplished since their father left and had sufficient time to do more before he returned with the rest of the family.

David began to think about the conversation he had with his cousin, William, when they met that first day on the trail. William had told him about the farm they had, the rich pastures, and plentiful wild game. He also recalled how excited Mary Jane was to hear that they were only about a day's journey away. With his work caught up and wanting to visit William and his family to see, first hand, what their life was like, David proposed that they pay them a visit; however, Mary Jane felt strongly that her responsibilities were to stay and take care of their new home.

David and Isaac made preparations to leave the next day and gave Mary Jane assurance they would return in three to four days. She agreed and was happy to have some time alone to really tidy up the cabin. And, too, she felt safe because she had not seen another hunter passing through since she arrived here nearly five months ago. Plus, she could fire a rifle with accuracy to ward off any threatening animal that might attempt to do her or their livestock harm. She stood by the cabin and waved good-bye to her brothers as they faded out of sight riding double on the horse, with Isaac holding on behind David.

Now, at the age of fourteen, Mary Jane was alone in the Appalachian frontier with the nearest neighbor a full day's journey away through some of the most rugged country known at the time. Yet, she did not feel alone or afraid. Instead she felt safe and secure as she had become familiar with the surroundings since arriving there in May.

She had finished feeding and securing the animals in their pens and was immersed in the beauty of the sunset and lush green hills that surrounded her. The warm evening sun was fast disappearing over the southwestern hill that rose in front of the cabin by the steady flowing stream. Her immediate world had a quiet and pleasant air about it that caused her to pause to enjoy this special moment before entering the cabin to prepare supper and retire.

Upon entering the cabin, she immediately barred the rather skimpy door with two hand-hewn oak timbers by placing them in the hooks across the entrance. This would certainly keep out the panthers, bears, wolves, and mountain lions that were plentiful and prowled the area.

She quickly began preparing the wild meat stew that had been warming over the fire. It would soon get dark in the cabin which had only one oil lamp and an open fire to provide light. She didn't bother lighting the wick because lamp oil was a scarce product and had to be preserved as much as possible for the upcoming long winter evenings. After finishing the stew and washing the bowl and spoon in the pan of water sitting on the hearth, she placed them on the table to dry. Then she added a couple of large logs on the fire to burn throughout the chilly October night and donned her gown to go to bed before dark arrived.

Her father and brothers had made beds of rough hewn walnut timbers for both bedrooms and crossed them with hand chiseled boards about two feet off the cabin's floor. She had gathered straw to make the beds more comfortable for sleeping and her covers were brought from North Carolina. With supper finished and by the light of the fireplace, she crawled into bed and quickly drifted into a sound sleep.

Suddenly the eerie, loud scream of a panther woke her in the middle of the night. The high pitched, wailing cries were easy to recognize as she had heard them several times before. However, these seemed closer to the cabin than the others. She sat up in bed and reached for the rifle she had placed on a mantle just above her. The panther continued screaming and began circling the cabin. This caused her to wonder if it had been stalking her before she entered the cabin. As it slowly moved around the outside making its menacing cry, she quietly slipped out of bed, with the rifle in hand, and peered through the crevices in the windows and door to locate it in the darkness. Even though the October moon provided some light, she was unable to see it since its solid black coat blended into the shadows.

It continued circling and even came up to the entrance which was the only door to the cabin. She could hear it sniffing and clawing the boards that held the door together. She moved directly across the room to the far end, cocked the rifle, aimed it at the door and waited. Her only chance, if it entered, was to fire one deadly shot. If she missed, there would be little hope of survival from this vicious wild animal. After moving from one side of the door to the other and prowling between the creek and cabin several times, it gave up and made a slow retreat into the woods. As it moved away, it was issuing less menacing cries that eventually faded into low grumbling growls and then... silence.

After waiting several minutes and listening for sounds that might give evidence that it was returning, Mary Jane once again quietly moved to the front of the room and peered through the crevices again. Hearing no sound of the panther, she breathed a sigh of relief. It was comforting to know that the cabin was a secure haven from the wild animals that might make the same attempt again before her brothers and family returned.

She quietly put another log on the fire and made her way to bed. Putting the rifle in its place, she crawled under the covers and drifted off to sleep.

Mary Jane awoke at daybreak and was preparing breakfast when her thoughts wandered back to her home and family in North Carolina.

"Did her father make it?" she thought. "How were her mother and the other children?" "When would she see them again?" "How soon would her brothers return?"

Such thoughts kept coming until it occurred to her of the hardships and challenges her grandparents had told her about as they crossed the ocean and settled in the new and exciting land. With this she was boosted to carry on believing that if they succeeded in overcoming their challenges, so could she. And even though she had been seriously threatened by the incident the night before, it did not shake her confidence. Instead, it served to strengthen her resolve to fulfill her responsibilities to her family.

Chapter Seventeen

Delayed Returns

David enjoyed his visit with William and his uncle's family. He learned how they grew their farm into a productive operation capable of sustaining a large family. But after a few days, he wanted to find out why most of the settlers were passing through to Kentucky. So he decided to take a quick trip to investigate for himself. The next day he saddled his horse, leaving Isaac with Uncle James' family, and headed out across the mountain.

He rode all day through a very mountainous region until he happened upon a family whom he remembered William had mentioned when they met on the trail in North Carolina. It was the family of Robert and Elizabeth Fleming who had settled on Shelby Creek near the small frontier community of Pikeville. David became fast friends with their son, John Jackson, and spent most of the next two days talking about the surrounding area and making a quick visit to Pikeville.

During his time away, David often thought of Mary Jane being alone and of his responsibilities for the farm. When he and John Jackson returned from Pikeville, he began making preparations to leave the next day for Uncle James' place.

It took him until dusk to get to his uncle's place and upon arriving he announced that they had to leave tomorrow morning because they had been away longer than he promised Mary Jane.

They were up early, thanked his uncle's family for their hospitality, saddled the horse and left. David was quiet most of the way because he was worried about Mary Jane and the farm. If anything had happened to either one while he was away, it would be devastating to his father and mother. The closer they got to the cabin, the faster David nudged the horse on. His thoughts caused him to spur the horse into a faster gait until he came in sight of the cabin and began hollering for Mary Jane. He yelled out repeatedly before she finally stepped out on the porch and waved.

When David saw her he spurred the horse into a gallop and, as they entered the yard he brought it to a sudden halt, threw his right leg over the saddle horn, and slid off.

"Are you alright?" he shouted.

"Why, sure I'm okay," she calmly replied. "What are you so excited about?

"Mary Jane, I'm sorry I stayed away so long but, I just lost track of the days," he sheepishly admitted. "I even went into Kentucky to visit a family there."

"So how was your trip and how's William, Uncle James and his family?" she asked, unconcerned by his behavior.

"William is fine and so is Uncle James and the family. They really have a nice farm, but I like our location better because we have more open valleys than they do," David answered as he began to calm himself.

"And, who did you visit in Kentucky?" she continued.

David interrupted her, "I want to know how you made it and is everything here okay?"

"Of course, I'm okay. Can't you see?" she replied.

"Well, you look okay. How's everything on the farm?"

"It's fine, too. And, Isaac, did you have a good time?" she asked, turning to him.

"I had a good time, but I'm glad to be home," he answered with a smile.

"David, why did you go to Kentucky and who did you visit?" Mary Jane asked again.

"Do you remember when we met William on the trail and he mentioned that a family by the name of Fleming had passed by their farm going into Kentucky? Well, I decided to see if I might want to ever move there and went to check it out," David explained.

"Oh, I do remember him mentioning that family because I thought they might be our neighbors and provide us company," she nonchalantly replied.

"I happened to find them and they settled near a place called Pikeville," he said, "and I got to know their son, John Jackson."

"Do you think you might go live in Kentucky someday?" she inquired.

"I don't think so. It's too mountainous and not enough good farm land." David didn't hesitate in his response.

"If I had known you boys were coming home tonight, I'd have had a good supper prepared, but since I didn't know, you'll just have to eat what I fixed for me," she informed them. "Now, take care of the horse, wash up, and come on in to eat.

After supper was finished, they gathered around the open hearth and she told them about the panther incident and a few other occasions when she was visited by bears, wildcats, and even a pack of wolves. But, she scared them off before they caused any harm to her or the animals. Then she informed them that there was some hay to be put up and more late vegetables to be gathered to have for their family when they arrived.

It was mid October and their father had been gone just over two weeks. He told them before he left that it should take no longer than two weeks to sell their property, pack the family, and make the trip back. So they were on a constant lookout and expected him to show up with the family any day now. Another week passed and they were beginning to get worried that something had gone wrong, either with their father on his trip, or to the family, or on their way back.

As each day passed, Mary Jane continued to do what she could to improve the cabin while the boys worked on the out buildings and farm. They wanted everything to be prepared when the family arrived because the cold, winter months would soon come.

The end of October was approaching and they were beginning to worry that their family may not come at all and they might be left to survive on their own.

Mary Jane was in the garden gathering the last harvest of turnips and greens when she heard a faint sound of someone calling. She looked up and started walking in that direction. Then the voice got louder and she could hear others calling along with the noise of the horses and dray. She began to run when she recognized her father with her mother and smaller children following. With tears running down her cheeks, she ran as fast as she could to meet them. She was screaming as she leaped into his arms and quickly released him and ran to her mother. She clung to her mother not wanting to let go until her mother gently pushed her back to take a long, proud look at her daughter. Then she grabbed her mother again for a big squeeze and, still crying, she turned to greet her younger siblings.

She took Sarah, who was two years old, and started walking toward the cabin. The other children ran ahead.

"Where's David and Isaac?" Ollie asked.

"They went hunting early this morning, but they should

be back in time for supper," Mary Jane reassuringly responded.

"Then, they must be well?" Ollie returned.

"Oh, yes, Mommy. They're fine. We were beginning to worry about you and Pa because we expected you to be here a week or two ago."

"We probably would have but it took longer to get ready than we thought it would; and we were caught in an early snow storm at Shouns Crossroads. It was just too cold for the children to travel and we had to stay there three days before we could start out again," Ollie explained.

"I'm sure happy you're here now. Let's go see the cabin while Pa's taking care of the horses. I can hardly wait to show it you and hear what you think of your new home," Mary Jane exclaimed.

Chapter Eighteen

Welcome Home

"Pa, while you unhitch, I'm going to show Mommy the cabin," Mary Jane said, taking her mother's hand.

"Welcome to your new home, Mommy."

"Oh, my goodness, Mary Jane," Ollie whispered in surprise, "it's so clean and everything's in place. How did you do it?"

"Pa knew how to get things done and we just pitched in to help him," she replied.

"It's a lot more than I expected," Ollie continued, as she walked around taking it all in.

John joined the conversation as he entered the cabin, "Mary Jane, you children sure have done a lot of work while I've been gone."

"I'm glad you're pleased, Pa. We did our best to take to take care of it, like you told us to."

"What do you think of it, Ollie?" he asked, turning to his wife.

"I knew you all had been working hard all summer, but I had no idea the cabin would be this ready when we arrived."

"There's still a lot to be done. The important thing is we're all here together now and can finish it as weather and time permit."

Then he continued, "Well, all you've seen is the cabin. Come on outside and let's take a look at the rest of the farm."

Ollie's heart was filled with joy when she stepped outside and saw the children having so much fun after the very difficult journey from Spruce Pine. While John pointed out the gardens, Mary Jane told her about the vegetables they had preserved for the winter. They surveyed the pastures where the cattle and horses were grazing and the fields of fodder shocks and haystacks. John explained that the hogs were free to roam but would come when called. He continued to point out the landmarks surrounding their homestead and the large amount of uninhabited area between them and their nearest neighbors.

The tour ended when Mary Jane took note that evening was approaching and it was time to start supper. She escorted her mother back to the kitchen where they, once again, began preparing a meal for their family, as they had done back in North Carolina.

John unloaded the dray and placed each item in its place, either in the cabin or outbuildings. The children continued enjoying their games and exploring the creek.

The sun was beginning to go down when David and Isaac came in sight of the cabin. They could hardly believe what they saw. Children were playing in the yard and their father was herding the cattle and horses into the corrals for the night. White smoke was bellowing out of the chimney and the smell of food had drifted into the valley along the creek.

They started yelling and waving to their father. David coaxed his pack horse into a trot. John looked up when he heard them and recognize his sons.

"Ollie, come quickly," he hollered, "David and Isaac are here."

She burst through the door and came running toward her sons.

"Welcome back," she screamed.

John reached them first and gave them a "bear" hug

and said, "It's so good to see you boys again."

Ollie arrive just as John put Isaac back on the ground. She picked him up and swung him around before turning him loose and stepping into David's waiting arms. By the time she let him go, the other children joined to greet their brothers. It was a special family reunion since they hadn't seen each other for almost six months.

"How was your hunt?" John interjected.

"It was good. We left early this morning and found a flock of wild turkeys roosting in trees and got two before they flew. Then we killed a nice buck down by the Pound River. I figured since cold weather is upon us, we could cure the meat before it spoiled." David responded.

"We sure can and that will be some good eating," Ollie exclaimed.

Just then, Mary Jane came out to welcome her brothers back and told them to get ready for supper.

John went with the boys to hang the buck in a safe place and take care of the horse. Ollie returned to the kitchen to assist Mary Jane in finishing the meal and the children continued their games.

With his entire family gathered around the table for the first meal in their new home, John gave thanks to God and asked for His continued blessings on his family. Then, as they were accustomed, conversations turned to catching up on the happenings since they last gathered together in North Carolina. Needless to say, supper lasted much longer than usual. In fact, John had to light a couple of oil lamps for Ollie and Mary Jane to put the younger children to bed. They cleaned the supper dishes and continued their conversation. While John and the boys secured the deer for dressing the next morning, John wanted to find out all he could about the farm and if anyone had moved in near them. He was pleased to learn that their nearest neighbors were still his brother, James, on the headwaters of the Pound River and Dick Colley, near the Breaks.

As days turned to weeks, weeks to months, and months to years, John built a larger and more comfortable cabin for his growing family. He selected the site a short distance from his first cabin along the stream he called Holly Creek. Then he returned to North Carolina as soon as he had adequate living space and brought his father, John Wesley (Revolutionary John) Mullins to live out his life with him and Ollie.

As time moved on, John acquired a large amount of land surrounding his homestead.

(In "Pioneer Recollections of Southwest Virginia", Elihu Jasper Sutherland, Copyright 1984, presents the following statements relating to John's acquisition of land: page 52, Roland E. Chase is quoted on October 22, 1921, "Mr Mullins laid claims to about 10,000 acres of land around Clintwood. He had no deed for it, but no one interfered with his claim. He later sold some of it, but for the most part divided it up among his children, his youngest son John retaining the old homestead."; on page 141, George W. Fleming, gave this account on January 23, 1926, "Grandfather Mullins owned at one time all the land from George's Fork Gap to Nickel's Gap, and between Pound River and Cranesnest River, and settled his children on it. He got it from the Warders - Bill Aston was their agent."; and, on page 412, Simpson Holiday Sutherland gave this account of the Warders, "I have had several cases which involved the Warder land. They bought a large boundary from one Joseph Smith of London, and this tract was separated from the French (Tubeuf) land by the Alexander line.")

Most of their children were given surrounding farms as they married; however, some married and settled in

Kentucky and West Virginia. Also, they began selling their land to settlers who were eager to take advantage of the cheap, fertile land. Families, of such well known names as Sutherland, Phipps, Vanover, Yates, Anderson, Chase, Buchanan, Hall, and Wright, purchased land and moved to the area. A small community, first called Holly Creek, began to develop with the steady increase of settlers during the first twenty years following 1829.

John and Ollie had achieved their hopes and dreams of owning that piece of virgin land where wild game was plentiful, farm land was fertile, their children prospered, and they had experienced freedom and independence. Now, in their latter years, as they watched their grand children and great grand children grow up, they looked back with satisfaction and peace. They lived contented lives on their homestead, until their deaths, knowing that they had paved the way for future generations.

Family Record of John Mullins and Ollie Cox Mullins:
David Mullins
1810 - 6/29/1888; married Ruth Buchanan
Kizzie Mullins
1812 - ? ; married Lewis Cook, lived in NC
Nancy Mullins
(no record), died young in NC
Jane (Jennie) Mullins
1814 - ? : married Peter Mullins, lived in WV
Mary Jane Mullins
5/15/15 - 10/6/1893; married John Jackson Fleming
Isaac Mullins
4/12/1817 - 6/18/1886; married Elizabeth Mullins
Solomon Mullins
4/6/1818 - 11/8/1886; married Elizabeth Hall

James Mullins
1821 - 12/24/1878; married Elizabeth Wright
Hannah Minerva
1824 - ? ; married Phillip Fleming
John H. Mullins
11/22/1825 - 12/17/ 1902; married Mary Polly Bentley
Harmon Mullins
1826 - 4/3/1860; married Dicy Keel
Sarah (Sallie) Mullins
9/6/1827 - 7/15/ 1849; married Francis B. Greear
Ollie Mullins
2/5/1832 - 2/10/1910; married Eli Vanover
Hazy Mullins
5/16/1834 - 12/12/1902; married Jacob Yates

Burial site of John Wesley Mullins
"Revolutionary John"
On hill across from the Chevrolet garage, Clintwood, VA

Burial site of John Mullins and Ollie Cox Mullins
Just off High Street in Clintwood, VA

Chapter Nineteen

Pioneer Lady

1830 came and went with improvements to the cabin and more fields cleared, plowed, planted, and harvested. Their farm animals had increased and sheep added. They had survived their second winter without mishap and spring of 1831 was just around the corner.

Mary Jane continued to assist her mother with the many tasks required to care for a large family. She helped prepare meals and cleaned the cabin. She took care of the needs of the smaller children and nursed them through sickness to health. She boiled clothes in large tubs on open fires and scrubbed them on washboards in the creek. She mended clothes and spun wool. She planted gardens and gathered and preserved fruits and vegetables. She did whatever was necessary to provide the most comfort for her family, especially her mother. The work was hard and the days long but she didn't complained. Instead, she cheerfully went about her tasks, knowing that when she had her own family, she would be well prepared to give them her best.

In the interim, David and John Jackson Fleming had visited each other several times in the winter months when work was slow. During one of his early visits, John Jackson took notice of Mary Jane, who was maturing into an attractive young lady. He visited her as time permitted and began a courtship. Then following the harvest season of 1832, at the Mullins family's Christmas dinner, he proposed to her and asked her parents' permission to be married. They consented.

In late January, 1833, John Jackson took his bride-to-be, on horseback, to introduce her to his family on Shelby Creek, near Pikeville, Kentucky. They were married in Pikeville on January 31, 1833 and made their first home on Jack's Fork of Big Beaver Creek in Floyd County, Kentucky. In 1834, they moved back to her parents' farm in Russell County, Virginia where their first child, John, was born. They were given a large tract of land by her parents just north of Holly Creek to establish their homestead. *(Now known as Flemingtown.)*

In the brief period of five years, Mary Jane had made the difficult journey from Spruce Pine, North Carolina to Holly Creek in Russell County, Virginia. She was a major contributor in establishing her parents homestead. She had survived being left alone in the wilderness. She had learned the lessons of being a wife and mother on the frontier. She had married, lived in Kentucky for over a year, was pregnant with her first child, and moved back to Holly Creek to start over again. She and John Jackson built their own cabin, cleared fields, plowed, and planted gardens and crops just like she had done before.

They, too, witnessed the steady growth of Holly Creek and the surrounding area. By the 1850's, Holly Creek had grown into a sizable community, Wise County had been formed from Scott and Lee counties, and rumors were circulating that it was nearing time to form another county to serve the area surrounding Holly Creek.

Also, during this period of immigration, John Jackson and Mary Jane made their contribution to this expansion with the birth of their twelve children from 1834 to 1859.

Then in the 1860's, with the entire country embroiled in a vicious Civil War, John Jackson enlisted in the Confederate army and was engaged in several minor battles and skirmishes. Their son, Isaac, also enlisted in the Confederate army and was killed in the war. As in most communities throughout the country, neighbors and families were divided on the issues of the war and this area was not spared from these divisions.

Mary Jane Mullins Fleming and John Jackson Fleming were married forty eight years. She lived seventy eight years. John Jackson lived sixty six years. They both lived to witness the eventual growth and formation of Dickenson County from Russell, Wise, and Buchanan counties by the Virginia General Assembly in 1880. It was named for William J. Dickenson, a member of the Virginia House of Delegates from Russell County and descendent of Henry and Elizabeth Dickenson from Dickensonville. The first county seat of government was located in Ervington but moved to Holly Creek in 1882 and the name changed to Clintwood in honor of Major Henry Clinton Wood.

**Family Record of John Jackson Fleming
and Mary Jane Mullins Fleming:**
John Fleming
born Aug. 29, 1834, Russell County, VA, died 1912, married Mary Francis Adams. No children
Lavina/Melvina Fleming
born Mar. 1836, Russell County, VA, died 1906, married 1) Marshall Keel; 2) John Counts
Isaac Fleming
born 1838, Russell County, VA, never married, killed in Civil War
Emmanuel "Manuel" Fleming
born May 12, 1840, Russell County, VA, no death date, married Margaret Elizabeth Mullins
Martha Fleming
born November, 1842, Russell County, VA, died April 11,

1925, married Wesley Y. Vanover

Sarah Fleming
born 1846, Russell County, VA, no death date, married Frank Taylor

William Jefferson Fleming
born December 9, 1846, Russell County, VA, died June 30, 1921, known as "Crippled Billy", married Martha Jane "Patsy" Branham

David T. Fleming
born 1849, Russell County, VA, died 1918, married 1) Mary Catherine Smith; 2) Sarah Harmon; 3) Effie Jackson

Robert Jefferson Fleming
born March 5, 1851, Russell County, VA, died 1907, married Mary Elmira "Polly" McFall

George Washington Fleming
born April 21, 1853, Russell County, VA, died December 29, 1937, known as "Cooley George", married Lucy Clevenger Ratliff

Mary Jane Fleming
born May 6, 1857, Wise County, VA, died September 28, 1936, married Frank Monroe Beverly

Andrew Jackson Fleming
born May 6, 1859, Wise County, VA, died October 5, 1901, married Florina Senter.

During her lifetime, Mary Jane had experienced the trials, tribulations, and harshness of a pioneer's existence and, throughout, exhibited the true pioneer spirit worthy of an honored position and due recognition by her descendants and community.

On October 9, 1993, Mountain People and Places, gathered at The Johnny B. Deel Memorial Library in Clintwood to pay tribute and honor Mary Jane Mullins on the one hundredth anniversary of her death.

*Burial site of Mary Jane Mullins Fleming
and John Jackson Fleming
Flemingtown Cemetary*

*Foot marker of John Jackson Fleming
Flemingtown Cemetary*

Pioneer Lady monument at the Johnny B. Deel Memorial Library

Mary Jane Mullins carried this gourd from North Carolina in 1829 to Holly Creek. She gave it to her son, Robert Jefferson Fleming, who gave it to his son, Samuel J. Tilden Fleming, who gave it to his daughter, Lilly Fleming Sowards, who gave it to Darrell R. Fleming. Lilly F. Sowards was told that Mary Jane kept sulphur in it. Lilly said the corn cob and cloth were in the gourd when she received it.

Darrell presented the gourd at the unveiling ceremony of the **Pioneer Lady** monument. He later donated the gourd to the Dickenson County Historical Society. It is on display in the Society's museum in Clintwood.

*Betty Belcher wearing Mary Jane Mullins Fleming's bonnet with the author at the dedication of the **Pioneer Lady** monument.*